J.D. AND THE FAMILY BUSINESS

written by
J. DILLARD

illustrated by
AKEEM S. ROBERTS

KOKILA
An imprint of Penguin Random House LLC, New York

First published in the United States of America by Kokila, an imprint of Penguin Random House LLC, 2021

Text copyright © 2021 by John Dillard
Illustrations copyright © 2021 by Akeem S. Roberts

Visit us online at penguinrandomhouse.com.

Library of Congress Cataloging-in-Publication Data

Names: Dillard, J., author. | Roberts, Akeem S., illustrator. | Dillard, J.
J.D. and the great barber battle.
Title: J.D. and the family business / written by J. Dillard ; illustrated by Akeem S. Roberts.
Description: New York : Kokila, 2021. | Audience: Ages 6-8.
Summary: "Eight-year-old kid barber J.D. joins forces with his sister,
who has beauty shop dreams, to find stardom online"—Provided by publisher.
Identifiers: LCCN 2021002358 (print) | LCCN 2021002359 (ebook) | ISBN 9780593111550 (v. 2 ; hardcover)
ISBN 9780593111574 (v. 2 ; paperback) | ISBN 9780593111567 (v. 2 ; ebook)
Subjects: CYAC: Barbering–Fiction. | Haircutting–Fiction. | Video recordings–Production and direction–Fiction.
YouTube (Electronic resource)–Fiction. | African Americans–Fiction. | Mississippi–Fiction.
Classification: LCC PZ7.1.D5593 Jaah 2021 (print) | LCC PZ7.1.D5593
(ebook) | DDC [Fic]–dc23
LC record available at https://lccn.loc.gov/2021002358
LC ebook record available at https://lccn.loc.gov/2021002359

Book manufactured in Canada

ISBN 9780593111574 (pbk)   10 9 8 7 6 5 4 3 2 1
ISBN 9780593111550 (hc)   10 9 8 7 6 5 4 3 2 1
FRE

Design by Jasmin Rubero
Text set in Neutraface Slab Text family

CONTENTS

CHAPTER 1
Mom's New Hair

"J.D.!" I heard my mom yell out to me. "Come here really quick!"

It was the night before her college graduation. Her second one, actually. The first one was when she studied to be a nurse, but she wanted to try something else. This time, she went back to get a business degree called an MBA. She'd be starting a new job at the mayor's office.

I had a newish job, too, and I was only eight years old! After I won the Great Barber Battle of Meridian, Mississippi, a few months ago, I started working for the one real barbershop in town, Hart and Son. With the money I made on Saturdays, I bought candy and comics.

When I got to my mom, she was standing in front of the bathroom mirror. I could see she had thrown her entire box of hair supplies in the trash.

"J.D., I want you to give me a haircut. I need a new look for my new job. And I want to look special for my graduation. I'm giving a speech."

Mom had been chosen to be something called a valedictorian. It sounded like a special award for being smart, which my mom was. We were excited for her to finish school. She said her new job would give her more time with her kids—me; my older sister, Vanessa; and my baby brother, Justin. We all lived together with my grandparents, Mr. and Mrs. Slayton Evans, in a one-story house built in the 1930s. You'd think it'd be a circus, but it wasn't. The grown-ups kept us organized.

"How do you want to look, Mom?" I asked her.

Mom sat down on the stool we kept in the bathroom and pulled out her phone. She showed me a picture on Instagram of the lady who played Nakia in *Black Panther*. She had a short haircut with a part cut into the side of her head.

"I want that!" Mom said.

"Wow, Mom, really?" I'd only ever seen my mom with short hair, like her pixie cut, but this was SHORT.

"Yes, I'm sure," she replied. "I figure it's something a barber can do, and I have the best barber in the whole city living in my house," she said proudly.

I went back to my room to get my clippers.

The buzzing sound they made when I turned them on always helped me focus and get into the zone.

As my mom's hair fell to the floor, I hoped I was doing a good job. I wanted her to feel special on her special day.

When I finished, I passed Mom a hand mirror, and she took a look. She touched her head, and her eyes got wide. Then they started to get glossy. She was crying.

Had I done a terrible job? Did she hate how she looked?

I'd never done a lady's hair before, and maybe I needed to practice before I tried cutting hers. I imagined Mom getting up onstage tomorrow and everyone pointing and staring. The last time I had a crooked fade, the kids at school made fun of me for weeks! What had I done?! Now Mom would need to keep her graduation cap on the whole time!

Then her lips curled into a smile that changed her whole face.

"I can't believe how great I look," she said.

No one had ever cried in my barber chair before. Thankfully, these were tears of joy.

"And my son James is the reason why I look great!" she added.

I felt so good and warm inside. Now I was excited that my work would be on display in front of hundreds of people at the university auditorium tomorrow! Something like that hadn't happened to me since the Great Barber Battle.

After I won, people would fist bump me, let me cut in line, or give me free samples at the ice cream shop. There was even an article written about me in the *Meridian Star* newspaper. Granddad framed the article and hung it in the living room next to some artwork I drew. It was the best!

I had been wondering if I was losing my touch. I'd had to pay for my own ice cream for weeks. Was I being forgotten?

Mom gave me a tight hug and left the room beaming. At least she was still my biggest fan!

Granddad dropped Mom off early for her graduation rehearsal in the morning. That gave us enough time to prepare for Mom's secret surprise party.

"Okay, everybody, let's spring into action," Granddad told us when he got back to the house.

We put out a banner that said "Happy Graduation" above the back porch and used aluminum foil to cover the chocolate cake, fried chicken, and potato salad Grandma had made. Everyone who was invited was asked to bring an extra dish, and I was looking forward to eating everything when we got back!

At the ceremony, Mom looked so confident in front of the audience with her new haircut. Her earrings glistened as she talked. But it was hard to concentrate on what she was saying because I got so hot sitting there in my church clothes.

The good thing was that not only was Mom out of school, so was I! Summer vacation was about to start. Well, Douglass Elementary School was about to finish up, but the Evans Summer School program would be in full effect.

"Granddad, aren't I going to learn this stuff next

year?" I had asked him when he gave me a sheet of paper with every subject he, my grandmother, and Mom planned to go over with me and my sister this summer.

"It's better to be ahead than behind," he had said.

I guess he was right, but just once I'd like to be able to do nothing but swim, play video games, and eat ice cream until school starts!

"And last, but not least, please clap for our final graduate, Mr. Harold Zeet!"

I felt a tap on the back of my head as Mr. Zeet smiled and grabbed his diploma.

It was Vanessa. She handed me a piece of paper. It read:

I have an idea for how to have the best summer ever.
Let's talk at the party.
This deal will expire, so don't miss out!

My sister had a huge grin on her face. She only smiles like that when she's up to something. Like the time she got the idea to sneak out of church and go home to finish watching *The Mandalorian* after our friend Jessyka shared her Disney+ password with us. Vanessa timed it perfectly so we could get back before anyone knew we were gone.

What did she have in mind this time, and how much trouble would we get in?

CHAPTER 2
A Double Surprise

When the graduation ended, we told Mom we were going to the New Meridian Buffet, a restaurant that had become our favorite place to eat at when we took a day off from cooking.

As we drove past our house, Grandma said, "I forgot my wallet, Slayton. Pull inside and I'll come right back out."

But when we pulled into the driveway, everyone who had been hiding in the backyard jumped out and yelled, "Surprise!" My best friend, Jordan, and my other friends Xavier and Eddie were there. Vanessa had invited a bunch of friends, too, including Jessyka, who was friends with both of us. Jessyka was in my grade and on my peewee football team. She sometimes joined our lunch table when there was a new issue out of our favorite comic or when she wanted to show us a cool new YouTube video.

Mom was definitely surprised. And speechless!

We sat around and talked, ate, and danced to the playlist coming from Jordan's Beats Pill.

Vanessa walked over to me with Jessyka and asked, "Are you ready to hear my idea, J.D.?"

"I guess," I said. I wanted to hear the deal before it expired, like Vanessa's note said it would!

Jessyka smirked and pulled out her iPhone. She went to YouTube and typed in the words "child barber."

I leaned in, and we all watched as Jessyka scrolled through videos of kids with clippers in their hands, cutting grown people's hair. Some of the barbers were girls, some were boys, some were in other countries, but they were all around my age. I had looked at barber videos before to try to learn new styles, but never ones done by other kids.

"Hmm, all this kid is doing is a drop fade. I do those every week at Hart and Son, and I even do teardrop ones now," I told her. "That's not that special."

Jessyka continued to scroll.

"Why are you showing me this?" I asked them.

"This is what's going to help us save our summer!" Vanessa said.

I gave her a confused look. What did she mean?

"J.D., you just can't get it through your head!" Jessyka said with a laugh.

"Let's start a YouTube channel!" they exclaimed at the same time.

Then Vanessa picked it up. "If we put a girls' nail and hair salon together with boy haircuts, everyone will watch and we will get way more views than these other kids."

The confused look on my face didn't change, so she continued.

"We can become famous, and not just in Meridian!" she said. "This kid has over eight million views. There aren't even three million people in the entire state of Mississippi!"

We always had facts and figures about our state memorized, thanks to Evans Summer School.

"C'mon, J.D.," Vanessa said. "I can tell you're bored with Hart and Son."

It never seemed like Vanessa paid attention to

me or what was happening in my life, but maybe I was wrong.

"Okay, Vanessa, but who is going to film us? We don't know how to add music and edit videos like this," I said. "We don't even have our own phones because we're not allowed!"

Vanessa turned to Jessyka, who finally put her phone away.

"I know how to do it," Jessyka said. "I already started a channel for my track races."

Jessyka had shown me her channel before, and her videos did look like little movies. It was another thing she was good at. She would probably be president someday.

"Working together could be fun!" I said. "What else are you doing this summer?"

Last year, Jessyka came back to school having learned tae kwon do. She showed me a perfect roundhouse kick while I had on my football pads so it wouldn't hurt, even though it still kinda did. It was amazing!

"Wow, Jessyka, cool karate kick!" I had told her.

"It's tae kwon do," she corrected me. "Karate

is from Japan and is more about your hands. Tae kwon do is from Korea and focuses more on kicks."

"How did you know that?" I asked.

"It's called Google!" She laughed.

Before Jessyka could tell us about her plans for summer this year, Grandma yelled out, "May I have everyone's attention, please?"

She was standing on the steps of the back porch, looking out at us.

"Jordan, please turn down that music," she said to my best friend.

Jordan shut off the music completely, and that's when I noticed how many people were in my back-yard. There were folks from church, the rec center where my grandmother taught ceramics classes, Mom's friends from school, and my friends' parents.

Grandma was always the life of the party, so it wasn't a surprise to see her get up to say a few words.

"Veronica, I am so proud of you! You went back to school and stuck with it! I love you, your daddy loves you, and we all love you! Slayton, do you have any words to add?"

"No, honey, I think you summed it up," he said as he put his arm around Grandma.

There were claps and "Awwwwws" from the crowd.

People must have thought that Grandma's speech meant gift time, because a line formed by the back table, where boxes of different sizes piled up and an empty bowl filled up with envelopes. I wondered if Mom would let us open the boxes with her like we did on Christmas Day.

Vanessa took Jessyka's hand and started leading her to the food.

"Think about it, J.D." she said.

I walked over to Xavier and Eddie, my friends from peewee football, who had been sitting with Jordan and talking about a video game called Minecraft the whole time. Jordan had just gotten into it.

"Can I see your phone for a second, Jordan?" I asked.

Jordan handed over his phone. I typed in the words "child barber" just like Jessyka had done a few minutes ago.

"Look at these kids," I said. "They're famous for doing the same thing I do!"

"You're famous," Xavier replied. "Everybody saw you beat Henry Jr. at the barber battle. And he's a grown adult!"

"Yeah," Eddie said. "You're the man here in Meridian."

I think Eddie meant that as a compliment, but it didn't feel that way, and I wasn't sure why.

"I only had to beat one person in Meridian," I reminded them, "and nobody outside of this city knows what I do."

If I told them about how the perks of the barber battle were fading away and how it felt like people were forgetting about me, would they understand? I wish we were at the barbershop. It felt easier to talk there. I decided I would tell my friends anyway.

"Vanessa said if we made hair videos together more people could see the work we do." I said it in one breath.

Jordan looked at Xavier. Xavier looked at Eddie. Eddie looked back at Jordan. Were they ever going to say something?!

"You want to be cooped up with your sister all summer doing hair?" Xavier asked. It wasn't what I wanted to hear, but I was glad someone had started talking.

"Why not?" I replied. "Jessyka knows how to film videos."

Xavier groaned. During peewee football last season, he was a little jealous of the attention Jessyka got on the team because of how good she was. By the end of the season, though, it seemed like they had made up and even started practicing together.

"There's no kid in town working and making money like you, J.D.," Jordan added.

Jordan had a point. I could buy anything I wanted right now, like video games. I liked that. But something still wasn't right. I didn't feel like the best at anything anymore. Plus, Jordan didn't know how boring it could be at Hart and Son on Saturdays and how tired I felt at the end of my shift. I had some money saved up, and it's not like I hadn't lived without money before. Maybe the summer was the right time to try something new and spend more time with my friends.

A few hours later, when the sun started to go

down and everybody went home, I retreated to my bedroom. I had lucked out because my sister shared a room with Mom, and my brother Justin preferred my grandparents' room. I usually fell asleep pretty fast, but tonight my mind was racing. I knew that I wanted to join Vanessa and that I wanted a break from Hart and Son. But how was Henry Jr. going to take it?

When he threatened to shut down my bedroom barbershop last year, I imagined pouring blue Gatorade into the canisters he used to sanitize his hair tools.

If I told him I wanted to quit, would he use his neck strips to tie me to his chair so I couldn't leave?

Since I wasn't going to fall asleep anytime soon, I brought out my art pencils and a pad of paper. Drawing was something I did when I was excited, nervous, happy, sad, or angry. Tonight, I decided to think of what my YouTube name could be. I'd need something catchy so people would know what I do.

SCISSOR MAN
BARBER BOY

J.D. THE AMAZING BARBER BOY

J.D. THE KID BARBER ✓

That was it!

Maybe it was time for the rest of the world outside of Meridian to find out about J.D. the Kid Barber.

CHAPTER 3
Poof

Every Saturday, I'd do my morning chores, catch a couple of cartoons, and head to Hart and Son.

My family had taught me to always be on time. We had so many people, jobs, schools, and activities to keep track of and only one car, so if someone was late, it threw everything off. When I went to work at Hart and Son, I was always there five minutes before noon.

Hart and Son was owned by Henry Sr. and Henry Jr. Henry Sr. was a tall, skinny old man, maybe older than the Earth. He always reminded me of a tall blade of grass with square oversized glasses, a small, neat Afro, and cargo pants held up high with a belt. He worked early in the morning and would finish at noon on the dot so I could take over his chair. He cut mostly older clientele who he had known for years. Henry Jr. was shorter and rounder than his dad. He had offered me a job after I beat him in the Great Barber Battle.

"Have a good day, J.D.!" Henry Sr. said as he patted my head on the way out the door.

At the barbershop, people talked A LOT about sports. Meridian didn't have any pro sports teams. In fact, the whole state of Mississippi didn't have any. So folks in town always pulled for the closest option. Since it was summer, there was nothing more exciting to talk about than baseball.

"The Braves are in first place again!" I heard Mr. Thomas say. He's one of Henry Jr.'s regulars.

"Eh, they never get past the first round of the playoffs anyway," Henry Jr. replied. "I'm just waiting for my Saints to start back up."

I wanted to play little league baseball, too. But unlike peewee football, you had to pay for your equipment, and Mom had been on a budget when we first moved in with my grandparents and she became a full-time student again.

Henry Jr. was responsible for keeping the shop going during the day until it closed at seven. On a good Saturday, I would average around ten haircuts depending on what styles people wanted. A simple fade or Caesar cost seven dollars and fifty cents for a kid and fifteen dollars for an adult. But more and more, people wanted complicated styles with color, dreads, and designs. I knew how to cut designs, and I charged more for that. My designs would look great on YouTube.

My last client of the day was a kid named Kelsey. Kelsey was about to start high school. I knew who he was because he played rec football. In Meridian, there were lots of open fields, and spontaneous games of football with kids of all ages would just pop up. I liked playing against big kids because it made me better.

"Hey, Kelsey, what's up man? What do you want to do today?" I asked him.

"I want a number two, even all over," he told me, pointing at the numbered chart of hairstyles on the wall.

Kelsey had big waves in his hair. So all I had to do was put a size two guard on the clippers and cut in the direction his hair laid down.

As I brushed the hair off Kelsey's cape, I knew

my shift would be over soon and I'd have to talk to Henry Jr. I started to wonder if maybe I was making a mistake by leaving.

One of the things I liked most about working at Hart and Son was that Henry Jr. didn't treat me like a little kid. That would be hard to give up.

"Hey, J.D., are you going to have time to meet up at the field this summer?" Kelsey asked, snapping me out of my thoughts.

"Well, I hope so, after I get out of Vacation Bible School next week! But my Saturdays are kinda full now that I work here," I told him.

"Aw, man, that's too bad," Kelsey said.

"Hey, there's nothing wrong with making money!" Henry Jr. had been listening to us. "J.D. is already ahead of most kids his age."

He came over and clapped my shoulder with his hand.

"Boy, J.D., you are my first and best employee," Henry Jr. said as Kelsey put on his backpack and got ready to leave.

"All these years it was just me and my dad. So many of my barbershop owner friends in other cities tell me horror stories about how they hire folks and then the next weekend they are just gone, poof!"

I thought about what I had to say to Henry Jr. today. I'd be another poof to him soon.

"That's right, now," Mr. Thomas said. "These days, it's hard to find good help!"

Now my stomach started to ache.

"With these new apps and websites and things, it's like any barber can just promote themselves without having to work in a shop," Henry Jr. said.

I felt a lump in my throat. Could Henry Jr. read my mind?

I had forgotten about Kelsey when I heard a quarter land in my tip jar. "Thanks for the cut," Kelsey said. "Maybe I'll see you around this summer at the field, maybe not!"

As Henry Jr. finished up with Mr. Thomas, I cleaned up my area. *I've got this*, I told myself.

After Henry Jr. locked the door and started counting his money, he spoke up.

"It seems like something is on your mind, J.D.," he said. "You usually talk more when you're working."

"Yes, sir," I told him.

"Well, what is it?"

I turned over my tip jar and put the day's earnings in my pocket.

"Let me guess," he started. "I bet you want to be outside with your friends this summer, don't you? I know I did when I was a kid."

Maybe Henry Jr. COULD read my mind!

"Yeah, it's something like that," I replied.

Henry Jr. went on to tell me how much fun he used to have in the summers as a kid in Meridian—

hunting, fishing, and finding swimming holes.

"If you want to take the summer off to play with your friends, I'll understand," he said.

"Are you sure?" I asked. "I don't just want to poof, disappear."

Henry Jr. stopped sweeping up the hair around his chair and looked me in the eye.

"There will always be a chair here for you if you want to come back in the fall," he said.

"Thanks, Henry Jr.!" I told him. "I learn so much from you. You're an amazing barber and a cool guy." I paused as a worry came into my head. "Are you still going to be able to make enough money, though?"

"Little man, the shop has been here for over fifty years, and you've helped us bring in more people," Henry Jr. said with a laugh. "You go enjoy your summer."

And just like that, my schedule had opened up. It was time to try a new adventure.

CHAPTER 4
Kidz Cutz and Nailz

The official end of school marked the beginning of Evans Summer School, which included a full week of Vacation Bible School.

Even though our schedules changed during the summer months, we ate breakfast together every day. My grandma's breakfasts were my favorite, especially her eggs and toast, grits, and bacon. There would always be a pot of coffee for her and Granddad.

Then, we would break off into our routines. Granddad dropped Mom at the mayor's office, Justin went to the rec center with Grandma, and Granddad would return quickly to make sure someone was with us during the day while we did our weekly assignments. He didn't leave for work—selling burial insurance around town—until the late afternoon. He used to run a JCPenney, but after he had a heart attack, he switched careers.

"We're all going to die, right?" he'd say when anyone asked about his work.

When Granddad was in charge, he always tried to ambush us to see if he could catch us away from our books. He'd hide behind a wall and pop out with questions about whatever subject we were studying.

"Hey, kids! So . . . what's the answer to question four on page twenty of your Social Studies workbook! Do you know? Ten seconds to answer or no ice cream after dinner!" Granddad said that morning with a smile on his face.

Vanessa and I were at the kitchen table going over the Mississippi facts. I hadn't told her yet that I had quit Henry Jr.'s for the summer and wanted to learn how to make videos on YouTube with her instead. But first, one of us had to answer Granddad's question.

"Granddad, the answer is the mockingbird. That is the state bird," I said as he counted down to one.

"Great job, kids. You'll both get an extra scoop of ice cream tonight," he said before walking back to the living room to finish watching the local news.

"Okay, Vanessa," I said. "Let's talk about YouTube."

Vanessa didn't even look up from Granddad's homemade workbook.

I noticed she had a briefcase with her. It looked exactly like the one Mom got as a present when she started her new job.

"Where did that come from?" I asked her.

"Granddad got it on sale at JCPenney. It's going out of business, so it was cheap," she said.

First she copied me with doing hair, and now she was copying Mom? I bet tomorrow she would have on a full suit!

"You haven't said anything about YouTube until now," she continued. "And since you haven't given me an answer, I got started without you."

"Wait, what?" I said. Maybe I shouldn't have quit Hart and Son so fast.

"I'll show you later on the computer," she said.

When we finished that day, we gave our workbooks to Granddad, who checked our answers.

"Okay, you two, good work. You're free to go outside and play," he said.

"Can we use the computer instead?" I asked. "Vanessa is going to show me something."

Granddad sighed.

"I knew this thing would be the end of you wanting to go outside! You can stay on it for exactly one hour," he said.

Vanessa went straight to YouTube to show me the video she said she'd already uploaded.

The video was titled "TWO ZIGZAG CORNROWS AND THE BEST NAIL POLISH MONEY CAN BUY." I could see the date was last Saturday, so Vanessa had filmed it when I was out of the house working at Hart and Son! She knew she wasn't supposed to go into my room without me being there. I thought about telling her that her video title was too long.

She pressed play and the first voice I heard was hers.

VANESSA: Hi, welcome to Kidz Cutz and Nailz.
VANESSA: I'm Vanessa, and I do hair! You don't know me yet, but I'm going to be all over the internet soon. Just watch.

JESSYKA: And my name's Jessyka. I do nails! And camerawork. And editing. And peewee football. And track. And tae kwon do!

VANESSA: Jessyka!

JESSYKA: What? I do a lot!

VANESSA: Anyway, this is our model, Lisa. Wave hello, Lisa!

[Lisa waves]

VANESSA: So, if you're looking for a cute weekend look—stylish hair and unique nails—you're going to want to save this video.

VANESSA: Today, we'll be showing you how

to do two big zigzag cornrows with matching bobos on the end! After that, we're going to try the best store nail polish money can buy!

Then the video cut to a musical intro. Vanessa sang the first part. Vanessa was a great singer. Much better than me when I sing in the church choir sometimes. I wonder what else I don't know about my sister. In the two years she was alive before me, what did she do? She was alone at first, no Justin and no me. Just imagine only three people in a house—her, my dad, and Mom. Maybe she played basketball on a baby hoop or drew pictures all the time, too?

Vanessa narrated the rest of the video, and Jessyka's camerawork was solid, showing the back of Lisa's hair as Vanessa finished. The ending shot showed the three girls in a row, with Jessyka doing Lisa's nails while Vanessa did Lisa's hair. I had to admit, it looked cool. Vanessa had gotten better at doing braids. For summer, she had cornrowed the front of her hair and pulled the rest of it into a large puff.

VANESSA: And that's how it's done!

VANESSA: We'll see you next week, when we'll share new techniques and tips.

JESSYKA: Remember, we're all NATURAL at this salon!

VANESSA: If you liked this video, let us know by turning on your notifications and hitting that subscribe button below. [Vanessa points downward so it lines up with the thumbs-up button on YouTube.]

VANESSA AND JESSYKA: Byeeeeeeeeeeeee!

Jessyka was good at YouTube. I just knew it was her idea to get a shot of herself throwing a cheap bottle of nail polish in the trash before zooming in on the good ones.

"What do we do with TRASH?" Jessyka had said. "We put it in the GARBAGE!"

Vanessa was good, too. Even Lisa, who just sat there like a mannequin. It had to be hard to sit still for so long. That's why I was a little afraid to do girl hair.

Part of me was still mad that Vanessa had used

the name for my bedroom barbershop and just added "and nails." She kept copying me! And the girls had also used my room, cape, hair supplies, and barber chair!

But a bigger part of me was impressed.

They had added a bunch of hashtags under the video, like: #YouTubeKids #KidzCutz #HairSalon #KidsHair #KidsNails #KidStylist #KidNailTech #NailPolish #HairGel #JrMasterBarber #KidsHairstyles #Hairstylist #KidHairstylist #NaturalHairstyles #GirlsRuleBoysDrool. They already knew that hashtags help people find videos.

I was ready to join until I looked at the views.

"Vanessa, this was great, but you only have fifty-three views," I said. That was a long way from the other kids she had shown me at Mom's party. "You want me to quit Henry's so you can use up my stuff, and no one is even going to watch these things?"

"Calm down, J.D.," she said. "I'll get more views, you'll see!"

Vanessa grabbed a pair of sparkling gold sunglasses from her briefcase and put them on even though we were inside.

"Are you in or out?"

I was already in; I just hadn't told her. So I finally did.

"I'm in."

Vanessa's mouth broke into a wide smile. I don't know what I expected would happen—maybe that confetti and balloons would fall to the floor as soon as I'd said "I'm in"? But instead, Vanessa told me some details she had left out of her pitch.

"Good. You know, these videos will make sure I get accepted into the Junior Business Scholars in sixth grade next year!"

"What is Junior Business Scholars?" I asked.

Vanessa reached for her briefcase, pulled out a piece of paper, and handed it to me.

I read it in silence.

CALLING ALL FUTURE BUSINESS LEADERS!

Marigold Middle School's inaugural Junior Business Scholars program is for incoming sixth graders interested in starting a business and learning about entrepreneurship. Local business leaders will mentor a group of ten students throughout the fall semester. Students will learn how to turn their idea into a business plan, how to market it, and how to assess profit and loss. To apply, students must submit a new business idea that includes at least one employee. Turn in proposals to Principal Yip, at marigoldprincipal@meridiam.edu by July 1! Only ten students admitted per semester.

"So your business idea is to start a kid's hair salon just like I did?" I asked.

Vanessa scrunched up her face at me.

"No, not exactly. I'm going to become a *hair influencer*. People will view my videos and copy my hairstyles. It's all online," she said.

We stood there without saying anything for a minute. Finally, Vanessa took off her sunglasses and looked at me, eye to eye.

"Mom has a job, Granddad has his own business, Grandma teaches ceramics classes, and you work, too," she said. "I'm the only one without a job. Justin doesn't count."

"But how can you make money from that?" I asked her.

"Do you think all those YouTube kids I showed you at the party are working for free? Views equal money! Together, little brother, we're going to be rich and famous, and we're going to help people all over the world feel good about their hair."

I kinda felt tricked. Vanessa needed to do this for school.

But one thing I knew about Vanessa was that she accomplished anything she set her mind to. Whether this was for school or not, she'd take it far. Especially if we worked together.

CHAPTER 5
Vacation Bible School

"I can't wait to show you the new activities we have planned this year," Grandma said about Vacation Bible School. She was one of the instructors there. She even took time off from the rec center to devote to teaching the Bible to kids. Grandma knew more about the Bible than even Pastor Harris, I thought.

Vacation Bible School was in our normal church, Won't He Do It Missionary Baptist Church. I think the only reason they called it "vacation" bible school was because it was during summer. But it was mostly the same as the bible study we had during the school year. We'd eat breakfast, then split up by age groups and get a lesson on either the New Testament or the Old Testament. We had a brief recess, lunch, and then more lessons on the Bible.

And this year, me and Vanessa were in the same class.

None of my friends from peewee football, like Jordan, Xavier, Eddie, or Jessyka, had to go to Vacation Bible School. That meant lots of time with Vanessa.

"Does anyone know the difference between John the Baptist and John, the disciple?" Ms. Smith asked.

Ms. Smith worked at the local library. I wished Grandma and Granddad had been assigned to my age group, but I think they signed up to teach other kids on purpose.

"Once Vacation Bible School is over in a week, we'll have more time on our hands," Vanessa whispered as she leaned over to me. "We'll be able to work on our videos."

"I know," I said, "and I've been thinking about how to make them better. We need new, catchy names. I'm calling myself J.D. the Kid Barber. You can't just be Vanessa. That's boring."

Vanessa sort of scrunched her nose at me.

"YOUR name's boring," she said under her breath.

But later, when we were supposed to be

answering questions in our workbooks, I could see her writing new names all over the pages.

At recess, after Vanessa finished her double Dutch round, she ran over to me and said, "How about 'Vanessa the Kid Stylist'? It matches your name, which makes sense since we are brother and sister."

"NO!" I told her. "You can't copy me."

"Fine," she said. "That was my second choice, anyway. How about 'Vanessa Does It All'?"

"Now, that has a good ring to it," I said.

A lot of kids stayed at the church for a few hours after the day was done if their parents couldn't pick them up right after. Me and Vanessa stayed late because Grandma was one of the caretakers and Granddad had to bring Justin here from the babysitter, pick up Mom, and head to his burial insurance visits.

We liked staying with the littler kids. The church basement had plenty of space to play hide and seek. And so did the sanctuary, where Vanessa pointed out the video equipment Pastor Harris used to record his sermons.

"I bet we could make a great video with that

camera, J.D.!" It sounded like she had already made up her mind.

Vanessa reached into the little purse she kept on her and pulled out something she called an SD card.

"Jessyka gave me this since I don't have a phone," she said. "The last time I was at her house, she showed me how her parents put it into their camera before they push the record button. It's blank, and she told me I could keep it so I'd be ready if I ever got a camera."

We stopped when we heard some sniffles coming from the corner. A little girl named Kay Kay was sitting by herself with her hair unraveled.

"Do you need help?" I asked.

Kay Kay told us that her barrettes fell off while she was playing, and she couldn't find them. They were shaped like bumblebees.

"My bumblebees flew away," she said, her shoulders sinking.

"I can fix your hair!" Vanessa said.

"But my barrettes are LOST!"

"Hold on," Vanessa told her. "Let me go get my brothers."

Vanessa asked me to go get Justin, who was playing tag. We'd need his help.

"J.D., I am going to fix Kay Kay's hair and I want you to record it," she said. "I just need fifteen minutes in the sanctuary with that camera. Justin can be our lookout."

I was shocked. Wasn't this lying somehow? It was definitely sneaking.

"Are you serious, Vanessa?"

"Don't be so scared all the time, J.D.," she said. "Trust me."

She walked by Grandma casually, like she wasn't about to tell a big lie. At church!

"Grandma," she said. "Me, Justin, J.D., and Kay Kay are going to go outside and play in the back for a bit."

Half the kids during after care would stay inside and play tag or board games, while the other half would go outside behind the church for football or double Dutch.

"Okay," Grandma told us. "I'll come outside and get you when Granddad has come back with your mom."

Vanessa nodded in the direction of the stairs. It was her way of telling me to go to the sanctuary while the three of them headed outside. I understood that my job would be to open the door from the inside after the other three walked around to the front of the church and knocked.

I heard Vanessa knock, and I opened the door. She was carrying Justin in her arms.

"Justin, I'm gonna give you a job," Vanessa said.

"Okay!" Justin nodded. He liked when we included him. He was a great helper, too. He was my very first client and barber assistant.

"Me and Kay Kay are gonna go into the sanctuary with J.D. I need you to stand on this chair and look out the window. If you see someone coming, just yell "Amen!"

Vanessa reached for a stray chair, gave Justin a Spider-Man figure that she had in her purse, and stood Justin on top of the seat.

This was getting scary!

"Do you think you can remember that?" she asked.

"I think so!" Justin said.

"Good," Vanessa said. "Me and Kay Kay will be right behind you."

My heart pounded a little bit. No one was allowed to be in the sanctuary during Vacation Bible School, not even teachers. They wanted it to stay extra clean and neat for Sunday service.

Vanessa moved like someone who knew what they were doing. It was always like that.

She walked over to the camera that was behind the last pew on the right side of the sanctuary. She removed the SD card that was already inside the camera and put in Jessyka's.

"Kay Kay, come sit on this stool and I'll fix your hair," she said. "J.D., make sure I'm in the frame and hit the record button."

Was this really a school project Vanessa wanted help with, or was this just an excuse to boss me around all summer? How was I going to become famous standing behind the camera instead of in front of it?

I walked over to the camera and looked at the screen to make sure Vanessa and Kay Kay were on it. When I pressed record and pointed at Vanessa, she jumped right in.

VANESSA: Hi! This is Vanessa Does It All again!

VANESSA: Have you ever had a hair emergency? My little friend here lost her barrettes, but I'm going to show her, and you, how to turn a hair emergency into a great hair day!

Vanessa pulled out a comb and went to work. She parted Kay Kay's hair in the back and made two even braids up the back of her head. Next, she took one of the rubber bands that held Kay Kay's unraveled twists and pulled the front of her hair into a spongy, bouncy puff.

VANESSA: Ta-da! That's your micro-video for today. This emergency is over!

VANESSA: Bye-byyyeeeeeeeeeee!

I took that as a sign to turn off the camera. Vanessa came over to remove her SD card and put the pastor's back in.

"Kay Kay, do you like your hair?" Vanessa asked, pulling out a mini mirror from her purse.

It seemed like she had a whole mini beauty supply store in that bag.

Kay Kay nodded happily.

"Good," Vanessa said softly. "Now, let's go before Grandma comes looking for us."

It was a good thing she was done. Justin wasn't even looking out the window anymore. He was just sitting on the chair shooting fake spider webs out of his wrist. Some lookout!

Back outside, Vanessa and Kay Kay jumped right into double Dutch without missing a beat while I stayed with Justin.

We had another video. But I wasn't even in it!

CHAPTER 6
The Cutting Room Floor

We did not film another video until after Vacation Bible School was over a week later. I told Vanessa I thought it was too risky.

"You're just a big scaredy-cat!" she said.

But I wasn't! The summer before, I got caught sneaking off to Jordan's house during recess, and I had to copy pages out of an encyclopedia for two weeks straight. Granddad had a whole collection of them, and that was his favorite punishment. I didn't like it because my hand hurt, but I did learn some interesting facts.

We returned to our regular routine of homework in the morning before playing with our friends. Grandma went back to teaching art classes at the rec center and took Justin with her most days. Granddad still stayed home with us until around three o' clock.

Even though we spent a lot of time together, he never let me cut his hair, no matter how good I had gotten.

"Justin and Mom are satisfied customers," I told him. "Can I do you next, Granddad?"

"A man's barber is sacred, J.D., and I already have one."

Granddad drove just outside of Meridian every four to six weeks to get his hair cut. The barbershop was small, with only one barber. Once, when he took me, I had to wait with him all day! I never asked to go back. I could tell Granddad was just good friends with the guy and liked going to catch up. That's how I felt when my friends were in my chair.

When we were done with our lessons, we asked Granddad if he could drive us to Jessyka's house.

"Did you ask her parents?"

"YES!" we both shouted.

Jessyka usually wore her hair in two big ponytail twists during the school year. But in the summer, she got tiny little braids with beads attached to the ends.

"Now I only have to get my hair done every two weeks," she told us.

I thought it looked so cool. But when she told me it took six hours to finish, I thought, *I'll stick to doing short styles.*

"Guess what we did, Jessyka," Vanessa said while holding up the SD card. "We filmed a hair video at church."

"What?" Jessyka replied. "How'd you do that without getting caught?"

Vanessa explained the whole story. I started sweating again just hearing it.

Jessyka took us down to her basement, where her family kept their computer and video equipment.

"How do you know how to use this stuff, Jessyka?" I asked.

"Some of the girls from my coding club showed me," she said.

"Geez, how do you have time to do so much?" I asked.

Jessyka sighed, like she was wondering the same thing.

"My parents make a calendar each month, with different colors for each activity throughout the day," she said. "It looks like a rainbow."

I suddenly felt glad that I only had to cut hair, play football, and do homework. It left room for drawing. Those were things I liked to do anyway.

"My parents want me to try everything," Jessyka added. "I only like some stuff, though, like this."

I watched as she inserted the SD card into one of the computers. A few seconds later, our video started.

It was very echoey and pretty dark. It wasn't lit

like Sunday service, and I think the room was better for singing than talking.

"There's only so much we can do to fix this," Jessyka said. "I don't think it's going to be usable."

Vanessa looked disappointed. I was relieved.

"Vanessa, someone from church was going to see it, and then everyone would know we were in the sanctuary," I said. "Let's just film some more videos in normal places."

My sister shrugged.

"Let me show you something I've been working on," Jessyka said. She pulled up a bright gold logo that said Kidz Cutz Hair and Nailz!

"Voilà! This can be a part of our intro," she said. "What do you think?"

Me and Vanessa looked at each other, amazed.

"Maybe we *can* turn this into something big!" I said.

"Maybe?" Vanessa replied. "Forget THAT. This IS something big!"

"Jessyka, do you think you'll be able to work with us on this idea?" Vanessa asked.

"Well, I hope so. My dad enrolled me in summer tennis camp, but I don't really want to go," she said. "I'd rather practice adding special effects to videos."

Jessyka did look happier in this basement than I'd ever seen her.

"Well, tell him it's for school!" Vanessa said. "That's not really a lie. I want to submit these videos for the Junior Business Scholars Program. It's due in a month."

We clearly needed Jessyka's help. The video we did by ourselves looked terrible. We'd never get any views! Plus, I knew that working on videos made Jessyka happy. I hoped she could do it. But if not, we needed a backup plan.

CHAPTER 7
Lights, Camera, Action!

On Monday, I interrupted our kitchen-table lesson on the Mississippi state bird, flower, animal, and the history of the Mississippi Delta to share an idea for our next video with Vanessa.

"What do you think about this?" I asked.

I had written a little script on a piece of paper and slid it to her. The last time I was allowed to use the computer, I had searched for tips on becoming a good YouTuber, and one of the top suggestions was to write out what you wanted to film before you got started. There was even a template that showed me how to do it.

If I wanted to be in front of the camera, I couldn't wait for my big sister's permission. I had to write myself in.

J.D. THE KID BARBER
CUTS A HI-TOP FADE WITH A RULER
SCRIPT BY J.D. JONES

AUDIO	VIDEO
Hey, everybody, which one of my friends is going to win a free haircut today?	EDDIE, JORDAN, AND XAVIER put their names in a hat. We pull one out and the winner gets a special haircut by J.D. the Kid Barber.
Oh, look, it's (whichever friend's name was pulled out of the hat). Sit down and let's have a look at what J.D. the Kid Barber can do! Tell the audience what you want, bro!	J.D. sits the "winner" down in a barber chair. He spins him around three times and puts a piece of toilet paper around his neck and a bedsheet over his clothes.
A hi-top fade looks hard, but it's only three steps. 1) Pick out the hair as high as you can. 2) Take your barber shears and even out the shape all around. 3) Fade the sides and create an edge. Then I have my special trick: a ruler!	J.D. picks out the winner's hair and blow-dries it. Then he begins to shape the hi-top with a trimmer.

And for extra credit, you can cut a design! Start with lines and half moons, and soon you'll be up to Marvel characters or whatever else you want.	J.D. begins to sketch out a design with his edger.
I'm done!	J.D. fills in the design with a colored pencil.
That's J.D. the Kid Barber, signing off!	Everyone jumps up and down and congratulates J.D. on a job well done.
	THE END.

Vanessa read the script in silence and then turned to me to make a face.

"Where's my part?" she asked.

"Well, the video you shot in church was all you!" I said.

"We had no choice in church because no one else could be the director except you! We'll have extra help so we can both be in the next one. The whole point of us doing these videos together is so we can get boys *and* girls to watch our channel," she said.

I still wasn't sure how we could make a good video with the two of us. Wouldn't it be really long?

"How about we alternate videos? One week it's you, one week it's me."

She didn't look convinced, and I knew I had to think of something else fast.

"Remember, I left my job at Hart and Son for this. If no one starts watching our channel, I'm going to go back to work. I don't want to be behind my friends in their comic collections."

I crossed my arms at the end for emphasis.

Vanessa sighed.

"Fine," she said. "My first video with Jessyka and Lisa is already up, and this week we'll add your idea. But don't forget who started this whole You-Tube channel!"

"And don't you forget that you got this whole hair idea from me! I won the Great Barber Battle!"

"I always did my own hair!" she said. "Even before you were born!"

We were getting pretty loud, and Granddad called for quiet from the other room.

"Okay, kids, I think you need a pop quiz!"

I didn't even have time to figure out how he snuck up behind us before he asked, "What's the state flower and animal—in that order please, J.D."

I took a deep breath. I had spent all morning writing my script!

"The state flower is . . . the magnolia. The state animal is the . . . owl."

Vanessa cringed.

"No, J.D., the state animal is the white-tailed deer," Granddad said. "Now, what's going on here that made you miss such an easy question?"

Vanessa and I were both quiet.

"You'll have to stay inside for an extra hour tomorrow with homemade flash cards," Grand-

dad said. He headed back to the living room, probably to continue his soap operas.

"Serves you right, J.D." Vanessa said.

"Whatever," I replied. "Now do you want to get everybody together to shoot this video or not? We'll see who ends up getting the most views."

To seal the deal, we shook on it.

Later in the day, we gathered our friends on the back porch and explained our idea for the video.

"Huh?" Eddie said. "I thought you called me over here to practice new throws." Eddie spent most of his free time playing football.

"Maybe if you learn how to do videos, you can upload your own football highlights," I said.

With that, Eddie was in.

"I'm missing Minecraft for this," Jordan said.

Minecraft was Jordan's new favorite thing to do.

"Jordan, you always said you wanted to learn how to make your own movies. This can be your start as a director or producer. Me and Xavier will be your actors," I said.

I knew my friend, and I knew this would get him excited.

"Here's the script I wrote this morning." I handed him a piece of notebook paper.

Not only did Jessyka have a stand for her iPhone, she even had attachments for sound and could angle the camera however she wanted. The daylight made the video extra clear.

I set up my barber chair and asked Xavier to have a seat.

"Hey, J.D., I think you should make some changes to your script," Jordan said.

I wondered if Jordan was just trying to give me a hard time. He was one of the main reasons I started cutting my own hair. When my mom tried to give me a fade and messed up my hairline, he told so many jokes.

"Look what I did." Jordan handed the paper back to me with notes and some lines crossed out.

AUDIO	VIDEO
Hey, everybody, which one of my friends is going to win a free haircut today?	EDDIE ~~JORDAN~~ (*I'm behind the camera*), AND XAVIER *wait for J.D. to pull one of their names out of a hat.* The winner gets a special haircut by J.D. the Kid Barber.
Oh, look, ~~it's (whichever friend's name was pulled out of the hat).~~ *XAVIER. (He has to win because he's the only one with enough hair. Just tell him to act surprised.)* Sit down and let's have a look at what J.D. the Kid Barber can do! Tell the audience what you want, bro!	J.D. sits the "winner" down in a barber chair. He spins him around three times and puts a piece of toilet paper around his neck and a bedsheet over his clothes.
A hi-top fade looks hard, but it's only three steps. 1) Pick out the hair as high as you can. 2) Take your barber shears and even out the shape all around. 3) Fade the sides and create an edge. Then I have my special trick: a ruler!	J.D. picks out ~~the winner's~~ *XAVIER'S* hair and blow-dries it. Then he begins to shape the hi-top with a trimmer.

And for extra credit, you can cut a design! Start with lines and half moons, and soon you'll be up to Marvel characters or whatever else you want.	J.D. begins to sketch out a design with his edger.
I'm done!	J.D. fills in the design with a colored pencil.
That's J.D. the Kid Barber, signing off!	Everyone jumps up and down and congratulates J.D. on a job well done.
	THE END.

"It's either that or the winner gets to choose his own style for you to do," Jordan said. "That adds a challenge."

Jordan was right. I knew he'd have great ideas! But I wanted to show off my ruler technique. I walked over to Xavier and showed him the new script.

"Do you think you can act surprised?" I asked him.

"What?! You mean like this?!" Xavier put his hand over his chest and started fanning himself like he'd just won the lottery. It was too much, but it worked. That gave me an idea for Eddie.

"Eddie, I need you to be real dramatic when you don't win, like fall on the ground or something."

"Got it." Eddie went down just like when he takes sacks on the field. It was hilarious!

"TAKE ONE! Jessyka, roll tape!" Jordan yelled out, clapping his hands together like he was using a real movie director's board.

I handed Jordan one of my Tuskegee University baseball caps. Inside, it had strips of blank paper since we already knew who the winner would be.

"Turn to the camera, J.D., say your name, and try to follow the script," he said.

"I'm J.D. Jones, aka J.D. The Kid Barber, and I'm the best barber in Meridian, Mississippi. Today, I am going to cut a hi-top fade!"

I closed my eyes, reached into the hat, and pulled out a paper.

"The winner of the free haircut is my friend Xavier!"

Xavier pumped his fists in the air and strutted over to claim his prize as Eddie crumpled to the ground in fake agony. I had asked Vanessa to be in charge of the props for this video.

"Vanessa, toss me a hair dryer!"

A dryer with a comb attached would make Xavier's hair stand up really high.

Xavier had a lot of hair. After I blew his hair up into a tall square puff, I created my guideline, faded his hair, and then edged him up. When I was done, I checked if his hi-top was even. I pulled out the ruler that I used for school and laid it on top to make sure it was even all the way across. It was perfect.

"Now, big sister assistant," I said, changing my voice to sound like a football announcer, "pass me my set of art pencils."

I don't know why my voice came out like that, but I went with it! I didn't really follow my script, either. It was like everything changed when the camera turned on!

"I'm not your assistant!" Vanessa rolled her eyes as she handed me the pencils.

I carved the word *Stylin'* into the back of Xavier's head and alternated the colors crimson and gold, Tuskegee University colors.

"Voilà!" I said. "I'm J.D. The Kid Barber, and that was another perfect cut!"

Jordan and Eddie jumped up and down and patted me on the back and head. They gave me high fives like I had just scored a pick-six!

"Okay, I'm stopping the video before I run out of memory," Jessyka said. "And Jordan, directors are not supposed to jump into the movie."

Jordan wouldn't stop jumping, though.

Vanessa sighed loudly and then laughed when Jordan bumped into her.

"I'm going to go home and edit this with my mom," Jessyka said. "I'll call you tomorrow when it's finished!"

I had done it. I had made my first YouTube video!

"Oh man! I wonder how many views I'll get, Vanessa," I said to her as Jessyka sprinted off the back porch.

"Well, we'll see how many *I* get when I make my next one with me front and center again!"

CHAPTER 8
Legend Only in My Own Mind

The next day, I was so eager for Jessyka to call us that it was hard to sit still. At breakfast, I played with my bacon, flipping it back and forth with my fork.

"Hey, J.D., are you planning to eat that bacon or just flip it until it's cold?" Granddad asked. "If you need an outlet for your energy, I'll gladly teach you to cut the lawn," he said.

For Father's Day, Mom had bought Granddad a motorized lawn mower. He had used a manual one for years, but when my grandmother inherited her brother's lot next door, adding lots of extra grass, my mom wanted to help Granddad.

"Thanks, baby. I hope this new machine doesn't make it too easy!" Granddad had said. He liked to do yardwork to keep in shape, he told me, especially after he'd had a heart attack a couple years ago.

I bit into a strip of bacon and watched Mom gather her things for work. That's when the phone rang!

"Hello, Jessyka," Mom said. "Would you like to speak to Vanessa?"

Mom handed the old cord phone to Vanessa. The cord was so long that Vanessa could sit in the living room to take her calls. One night, I almost tripped over it on my way to the bathroom when Vanessa stayed up past bedtime!

"Really, it's already done?!" I heard Vanessa say. "That's great!"

When she hung up, Vanessa told me my video from yesterday was live on YouTube. We still had to do our morning homework, but Vanessa said we could sneak on the computer when Granddad went to drop off Mom at work.

"But Vanessa," I said, "we aren't supposed to go on the computer without someone watching us!"

Vanessa sighed.

"It will only take a few minutes, J.D. I memorized the password."

»»«««

Vanessa laid out our multiplication workbooks on the kitchen table so they would be open in case Granddad came back early.

"I'll just do a few of your math problems first so it looks like we've been working," Vanessa said. "It's fourth-grade math. I already know it."

I didn't need her help. I was really good at math.

When I was done, I moved like a secret agent into the living room.

"Why are you tiptoeing, J.D.?" Vanessa asked, walking like normal. "No one is here."

Even though there was no one home to catch us, we knew we had to be fast. I sat by Vanessa at the computer, my palms sweaty. She was as cool as a cucumber, as my grandmother would say. I don't know why it seemed so much easier for her to break the rules! I thought back to her telling me to not be a scaredy-cat.

"There it is!" Vanessa said, pointing to the screen.

The video was about ninety seconds long. Wow, that was short! We had been outside filming all day.

Jessyka had added some cool special effects, like a floating title and some background music. Even though the shot was clearer, it still didn't look as good as some of the videos Vanessa had shown me of other kids on YouTube cutting hair.

I could see by the date that Jessyka had uploaded it the night before. It only had twenty-five views and no comments. I guess we had to give it time to get some more attention, but I was still disappointed.

A car pulling into the driveway snapped me out of my thoughts. Granddad was back.

Vanessa quickly turned off the computer, and we raced back to the workbooks waiting for us in the kitchen.

"I have a new idea for the next video," I told her.

"Well, it is MY turn to go next," Vanessa said.

Vanessa was busy doing math problems as if she had never left the table. Even though I knew it would bug her, I put my hand on her page so she'd look up and see that I was serious.

"That's part of the problem," I said.

Vanessa looked both surprised and annoyed at the same time.

"We need to do something really different," I said.

"Like what?" Vanessa asked.

"We need to do something together, at the same time. Like Chloe x Halle! They made a YouTube channel singing songs, and now they're famous," I said. "Jordan showed me their first real video because his brother Naija helped them film it when he was in college in Atlanta."

Vanessa smiled from ear to ear. I knew she liked Chloe x Halle.

"I think Naija still has some camera equipment in his old room," I said. "I bet Jordan would let us use it! He likes directing!"

"Wow, really?" Vanessa said. "If that's true, we just need to think of a really, really good idea for the next video!"

I was excited. Vanessa was excited. Now it was time to get Jordan excited to use a piece of equipment that didn't belong to him and that I had already promised we could get.

CHAPTER 9
Iron Man

Sunday was the only break we got from Evans Summer School. Today was Saturday.

"I'm glad we're getting back to our French lessons!" my mom said. She had already started teaching us the different sounds of the alphabet and the numbers one through ten. Mom knew French well, and even patois.

I wasn't sure when I was ever going to have to speak French, but it was easy enough to memorize the sounds, and I liked learning from Mom.

Mom asked us to pull out our French flashcards and quiz each other while she stepped out for a second.

Vanessa wasted no time sliding a piece of paper to me, grinning like she'd just won first place in her own hairstyling competition.

It was a new video script.

VANESSA DOES IT ALL'S BEADS AND NAILS

Script by Vanessa Jones

AUDIO	VIDEO
Hey, this is Vanessa Does It All here, and today we're going to do something pretty cool: match hair beads to your nails!	Jessyka sits in a chair and shakes her braids while she flashes her nails at the camera.
First things first: Remove your nail polish and take off your old beads. [Jessyka says] "Bedazzle me!"	Jessyka removes her nail polish and waves her fingers at the camera so everyone can see.
Let's see. With yellow beads, purple is the perfect complementary color.	Vanessa Does It All shows a color wheel to the camera and selects a purple nail polish from the table.
Now, for the bedazzle!	Little plastic beads are glued onto every other nail.
For the hair, this looks hard, but it's easy. I'll show you how to do two rows at home.	Vanessa takes down two of Jessyka's rows of beads and adds yellow beads.
That's all for today, everybody!	Jessyka shakes her hair back and forth as music plays.
	THE END.

I couldn't believe it. Vanessa had cut me out! I thought we had agreed that doing something together would get us more views. Instead, I was being forgotten again.

This wasn't the first time Vanessa completely ignored me. When I was younger, if she was frustrated with me, she'd pretend I wasn't even in the room with her. When I'd talk, she'd say something like, "The wind sure is loud today." Cutting me out of this video made me feel the same way.

"Vanessa, this isn't much of a family business," I said to her. "What happened to doing one together?!"

Vanessa took her script back and shrugged.

"I do have a part for you in this video," she said. "You can be the equipment assistant."

There was no way I was going to be the equipment assistant! I took her paper and started to mark it up. Jordan wasn't the only one with notes.

VANESSA DOES IT ALL + J.D. THE KID BARBER DO AN UNDERCUT WITH BEADS AND NAILS
Script by Vanessa and J.D. Jones

AUDIO	VIDEO
VANESSA: Hey, this is Vanessa Does It All here, and today we're going to do something pretty cool ~~match hair beads to your nails!~~ with my brother J.D. The Kid Barber! I'm going to match hair beads to our friend Jessyka's nails! And J.D. will give her an undercut with a design!	Jessyka sits in a chair and shakes her braids while she flashes her nails at the camera. J.D. spins her around in the chair and lifts her beads to show the back of her neck.
VANESSA: First things first: remove your nail polish and take off your old beads. **JESSYKA:** "Bedazzle me!"	Jessyka removes her nail polish and waves her fingers at the camera so everyone can see.
VANESSA: Let's see. With yellow beads, purple is the perfect complementary color.	Vanessa Does It All shows a color wheel to the camera and selects a purple nail polish from the table.
VANESSA: Now, for the bedazzle!	Little plastic beads are glued onto every other nail.

VANESSA: For the hair, this looks hard, but it's easy. I'll show you how to do two rows at home. **J.D.:** That might be easy, but an undercut is hard! You have to pay attention. Barber's assistant, Justin, please hand me my clippers! What style do you want in the back, Jess? [Jessyka answers.]	Vanessa takes down two of Jessyka's rows of beads and adds yellow beads. Justin hands J.D. the clippers. J.D. stands behind Jessyka and starts cutting.
J.D. and Vanessa together: That's all for today, everybody!	Jessyka shakes her hair back and forth as music plays. J.D. spins Jessyka around as the camera zooms in on her design.
	THE END.

Not only had I written a script that gave us both time to shine in front of the camera, but I had even found a way to include Justin! Now this was a family business.

I waited for Vanessa to clap and cheer. Maybe she'd even thank me for saving her Junior Business Scholars application by never copying me again!

But all she said was, "Wow, you think Jessyka will let you cut her hair? Do you know how to do girl hair?"

"Yes," I said. "She used to ask me for designs during football season. And I cut Mom's hair."

"Okay, J.D., whatever you say." Vanessa shrugged again, but I caught the smallest smile before she turned to leave. I knew she'd like this idea!

With a new script ready, we just needed Jordan's directing skills and Naija's camera.

When I got to Jordan's house, he was sitting in his room in the dark, with Minecraft glowing on his screen. There were empty bags of chips everywhere, and it felt hot, like he hadn't opened his windows in a million years. I wished he would go back to NBA 2K or Madden. At least that was something I liked to play, too.

"Hey, Jordan," I said.

I asked to pause the game for a second because

I had big news that he wouldn't want to miss.

"We're making another video today at Jessyka's house. Want to help?" I said.

"Do you need me to rewrite another script?" he said, laughing.

I told him about the new script I came up with.

"That's fire, J.D.," he said.

Jordan was hard to impress, so I felt proud.

"Do you know what would make it even better?" I asked. Jordan shook his head. "You as director using Naija's fancy camera!"

Jordan stepped back and rubbed his chin, like he was letting the idea sink in. Before saying a word, he walked into the hallway and opened a closet. Inside the closet were action figures, tripods, a ring light, and lots of Halloween costumes.

"Whoa, where'd you get all this?" I asked. "This looks like Iron Man's closet!"

Jordan kept moving things around like it was no big deal.

The camera sat on a top shelf. It came with two clip-on microphones and a big, bright white light.

"This is it," Jordan said. "It's Naija's, but it's just

been sitting in here for months. He didn't use it much after he graduated from college."

It seemed wrong to let such a good camera sit in this closet when we could use it to film our videos.

"Do you think we can take it to Jessyka's house?" I asked.

"Probably not, but who's going to know?"

Jordan grabbed an empty gym bag from the closet and put the camera inside. He grabbed some other equipment from the closet, too. I had no idea what it was, but Jordan did. I could tell that he was already thinking of more ideas for our video.

When we got back to my house, Mom was at the computer finishing up the church bulletin she volunteered to work on. I asked her if she'd give us a ride to Jessyka's, even Justin. She asked if we'd finished our chores.

"Yes, Mom! I only had one left—that's un in French—and it's done," I said. The French worked, and we piled into the car.

Jessyka was waiting for us on her back porch, and she already had her beads and nail polish set up.

Today, her beads were red, green, and black. She was wearing a yellow tennis uniform.

"So you're really going to tennis camp?" I asked Jessyka.

"It looks that way," she told me. "My dad says Venus and Serena Williams are going to retire soon, and somebody needs to take their spot. But I'd rather work on special effects. My videos look almost as good as *Avengers: Endgame!* I just need more time to work on one thing."

Jessyka looked down at her feet. Her parents always had her enrolled in something new. She once told me that her dad got close to playing pro football. I guess he wanted Jessyka to be a pro, too.

"Forget about *Avengers: Endgame!*, Jessyka," Jordan said as he walked up with the new equipment. "This video will look better than the last Star Wars movie!

Jessyka squealed as she looked at everything Jordan had brought. She looked happier than after she'd scored a touchdown in peewee football!

"Do you know how to use this stuff, Jessyka?" Jordan asked.

"Yes, a little bit. I took a video-editing class last spring on the weekends when track finished."

Vanessa started passing out copies of our script to everyone. "Okay, let's get ready to work!"

I watched Jessyka as she read about her role this time. I got nervous. What would she think of the undercut?

"Wow, J.D.," Jessyka said. "Are you going to cut my hair today?"

"Only if you want me to!" I said quickly.

Jessyka read the script again and then jumped in the air and kicked her legs.

"Yes!" she screamed. "I want a rose design in the back of my head, and can you color it yellow to match my outfit?!"

"Sure," I said, relieved. I whipped out my colored pencils to show everyone.

Jessyka walked over to the camera equipment and explained the different settings to Jordan.

"I will put my iPhone on a stand so we can film from another angle, too," she said.

Vanessa and I clipped on our microphones. My sister looked at Jordan and said, "Lights, camera, action!" and clapped a real black-and-white director's board that Jordan had set on the table next to a bowl of yellow hair beads.

Vanessa looked at the camera and started our brand new video.

"Hi, I'm Vanessa Does It All!" she sort of sang out in her choir voice.

"And I'm J.D. the Kid Barber!" I added.

Vanessa followed the script until she started describing what I was going to do.

"And my baby brother, J.D., will cut a design into the back of Jessyka's head. My other baby brother, Justin, will be our shop assistant for the day."

I couldn't believe she called me her "baby brother" in front of my friends! How embarrassing!

When asked, Justin handed Vanessa the yellow beads. I watched as she took Jessyka's beads off slowly, one by one, and replaced them with the yellow beads. How could this make for an exciting video?

After Vanessa finished, Jessyka shook her head so fiercely that she looked like a yellow blur.

Finally, it was my turn.

"Now, Justin, please hand me my clippers," I said.

We followed the script, and Jessyka asked for a rose design, yellow to match her dress.

My heart started to beat a little faster when I turned on the clippers, like it did the first time I cut Mom's hair for her graduation.

I undid a row of braids in the back of Jessyka's head. Next, I added a number two guard to my clippers, and I went to work as several puffs of hair fell to the ground. It was easy to buzz the hair off and smooth down Jessyka's neck, but it took longer to make a rose.

I spun her around to face Naija's camera and

asked Justin to give me my yellow pencil. I felt so proud as I colored in the rose.

"I'm done, everybody!" I yelled out.

"And on to nails!" Vanessa yelled out next.

It took them about thirty minutes to finish. Justin sat there, mesmerized, until finally Jessyka got up and dangled her hands in front of the camera.

"CUT!" Jordan yelled out. Jessyka did a spin. I think she was happy with her hair and nails, because she couldn't stop smiling.

She walked over to the camera and took out the SD card.

"Are you sure this is going to look right?" I asked Jessyka. "It's really long."

"Just wait," she said. "You'll see when I finish editing the footage with my mom."

Jessyka was explaining the things she wanted to do with the video when we heard a loud boom.

The back porch door swung. It was Mr. Fleet, and he looked like he was in a rush. Mr. Fleet was a tall, clean-shaven man who kept a very neat fade all the time. He still looked like the best wide receiver in the state of Mississippi that he'd once been.

"Okay, kids, time to wrap it up!" he said. "Me and Jessyka are going to practice hitting some tennis balls so she's ahead of the other kids when she goes to camp!"

Jessyka looked disappointed as she told her dad that we had just finished filming a great video and she wanted to start editing it right away.

"Jess, once you're the number-one tennis player in the world, you'll be able to pay someone to make all the videos you want," he said, looking her directly in the eyes.

I tried to get Jessyka to look at me so I could tell her with my eyes that I was sorry, but she didn't look my way.

"Call your parents to come pick you up, kids," Mr. Fleet said.

Vanessa said she'd go call our mom. She took Justin and followed Mr. Fleet and Jessyka inside.

While Jordan and I waited outside, I grabbed a football from the porch and tossed it to him.

"I wanted to get the video up quick," I said. "Think of the followers we're missing out on!"

Jordan caught the football. "Just go do something else, J.D. It's still early. Maybe I can expand my map on Minecraft."

It felt like whatever magic happened during our shoot had disappeared.

How could Jordan move on so quickly? I took the ball and threw it fast at him.

Jordan missed the catch and started to trip backward. I closed my eyes when I heard a crash.

"Oh, man!" I heard Jordan yell out. "What am I going to tell Naija?!"

I opened my eyes and saw Jordan kneeling on the ground with the camera. I rushed over to inspect it. The lens was shattered to pieces! I tried to turn it on, but it wouldn't work. And on top of that, one of the tripod legs was bent.

At that moment, Vanessa came back with Justin.

"Oooooooooooooooo," Justin said as he pointed to the broken camera.

"What happened out here?" Vanessa asked. "Now I will never get my videos to look how I want for Junior Business Scholars!"

Jordan got up and scrunched his eyebrows.

"Wait a minute," he said. "So, J.D., you're doing this for some kinda homework assignment for your sister?"

"No, not exactly," I said, staring at my shoes. "Vanessa promised me we'd all be famous."

Jordan shook his head and let out a breath.

"Well, good luck with that," he said. "All I know is somebody is gonna have to pay for Naija's camera. Thanks A LOT, J.D. None of this would have happened if I had stayed back home playing Minecraft!"

A car horn beeped, and we knew my mom was here to pick us up. Justin helped Jordan shove the broken camera pieces into his gym bag. We piled into the back seat and didn't say a word on the way home.

CHAPTER 10
The Debt

It was extra hot inside church the next day. Or maybe I was feeling guilty about the broken camera. Did I even have enough money saved up from Hart and Son to pay for something like that? I bet it cost a lot of money.

While Mom and Vanessa sang in the choir and Grandma and Granddad did their deacon duties of leading the hymns before the pastor started giving his sermon, my job at church was to keep an eye on Justin.

"Good morning, parishioners!" Pastor Harris said as he calmly walked out to the podium. Pastor was a short, round man. He wore glasses and a deep crimson robe with a big cross on the back and long sleeves that flared out at the wrist. He wore his hair in a Caesar cut and had no facial hair.

Even though he spoke in a booming, deep voice, he was always friendly and smiling.

"Today, we are going to talk about LIES AND TRUTH!"

"Yes, Pastor!" everyone yelled out.

I shrunk down in my seat and started to sweat even more. Could Pastor Harris read my mind? What did Jordan end up telling Naija about the broken camera? Did he say it was all my fault? How long before Jordan's parents would call my house?

I'd surely have to go back to Hart and Son to pay for the camera . . . and probably worse!

Back at the house, my family ate piles of greens, cornbread, black eyed peas, and the baked chicken my grandmother had started making because the doctor told her it was healthier than fried.

"You're awfully quiet tonight, J.D.," Mom said. "Is something wrong?"

My mom's cell phone rang before I could answer. I couldn't see who it was.

"Excuse me, everybody, I'll be right back," Mom said, moving to the living room.

We were always taught it was rude to talk on the phone at the dinner table, so no one ever did.

Her voice was muffled, but I heard bits and pieces.

"Oh, really? Hmm, thanks for letting me know. I'll talk to both of them about it. Good night."

It didn't sound good.

When dinner was finished and I had scraped the dishes clean and placed them in the dishwasher, I tried to make a beeline for my bedroom.

"Good night, everyone!" I said.

"Hmm. It's not that late, J.D. I need you and Vanessa to come have a chat with me in the living room."

Vanessa and I turned and looked at each other. Vanessa rolled her eyes. *This is your fault!* she mouthed.

"So I got a call from Naija today, and he told me that you kids took his camera this weekend without asking."

I gulped, waiting for the rest of the truth to come out.

"And he said it came back broken! Can someone please tell me what happened?"

Since it was my idea to ask Jordan for the equipment, I decided I had better speak up. It wasn't Vanessa's fault. She didn't deserve to get in trouble.

"Well, Mom, it was an accident. Me, Vanessa, and Jordan were filming a video at Jessyka's house, and the camera broke while me and Jordan were playing football outside," I said. "Vanessa wasn't with me when we took the camera equipment, and she wasn't there when it broke."

Mom looked at me for a long time with a soft face.

"Why did you need the camera in the first place, J.D.?"

"We just thought having a better camera would make our YouTube videos look cool," I said.

Vanessa put both her hands up to her mouth, like I had done something shocking. I guess I just gave away our secret.

"What YouTube videos?" Mom asked.

Vanessa stepped in front of me, like she was trying to shield me.

"Mom, remember when I said I wanted to apply for Junior Business Scholars?" Vanessa asked. "Well, the career I picked is hair influencer."

"I could have sworn you told me you wanted to do a girls-and-boys salon," Mom said.

"Well, it is a salon, just on YouTube. J.D. is my employee. He's working with me instead of at Hart and Son. We're making videos with Jessyka." That was it. All of it.

For a second I forgot about the trouble we might be in, because I was mad she called me her employee!

"You know you should have been more clear

about what you were doing, Vanessa. I don't feel you were completely honest with me."

"I'm sorry, Mom," Vanessa said. "But I'm almost done with the project. I have to finish now. Can I show you what we did?"

Mom followed us over to the computer, and Vanessa pulled up our Kidz Cutz and Nailz channel. Vanessa played her the video of me giving Xavier a hi-top fade with a ruler.

Me and Vanessa watched Mom in silence as a smile crept across her face. We still only had a handful of views, but there were a couple of new comments.

"That's creative," Mom said when everything

WOW! That's pretty good for a little kid!

2 comments   SORT BY

That kid could shape me up anytime!

REPLY

REPLY

finished. "But, Vanessa, you should have told me that you were doing this with J.D., and J.D., you should have told me that you stopped working at Hart and Son. The internet is not always a safe place for kids. That's why I have the rule about having an adult in the room for your computer time."

I was hoping that after all that, she would've forgotten about Naija's camera!

"It doesn't matter that Naija's camera broke by accident—you still took it without asking. Someone has to pay for it," she said. "A new one costs a thousand dollars."

A THOUSAND DOLLARS?! It was hard to hear anything after Mom said that. But she explained that Mr. Mathews had decided to suspend Jordan's $50 allowance for ten weeks to pay for half, and I was expected to pay for the rest.

"James, you do still have some money saved from Hart and Son, I hope?"

I couldn't lie.

"Yes, Mom, I do, but not that much."

Since Jordan had been given ten weeks to pay off his part, I got the same amount of time.

"I'm sure if you go back to the barbershop, you can pay what you owe pretty quickly," Mom said.

My shoulders dropped. That was it. It was over.

I shuffled back to my bedroom. I needed to start counting!

CHAPTER 11
Back to Zero

I couldn't open my old sneaker box right away. It's where I kept my money. Instead, I started playing NBA 2K with the Cavs and LeBron James. Whenever I played, I put LeBron on my team, and I would pit them against the Showtime Lakers, my mom's favorite team, or the 1990s Chicago Bulls. But video games made me think of Jordan, and Jordan made me think about the broken camera and how much money I owed. So I opened the box and started counting.

$20 x 1= $20
$10 x 3= $30
$5 x 2= $10
$1 x 8= $8
Total: $68

My part of the camera owed: $500 - $68 = $432.

Should I just go back to Hart and Son to pay it off? Then I'd have hardly any free weekends left this summer! Maybe I should just go every day of the week. I bet Jordan wouldn't want to talk to me anyway since he probably blamed me for getting his allowance cut off.

I woke up the next morning with a copy of the latest Spider-Man comic on my face. That's another thing: No more new comics for the rest of the summer.

Every option I had was a bad one.

Usually at breakfast, Vanessa was buzzing with new ideas and plans, but today she just ate quietly.

"Jessyka is starting tennis camp soon," she said in a sad voice.

We watched as Granddad got up to drop off Grandma, Justin, and Mom like usual.

As soon as they left, Vanessa shut her math workbook and slammed her head on top.

"How will I apply to Junior Business Scholars

when all the project has done is lose money?" she said.

"Well, at least you didn't lose everything, Vanessa. All I know is that I have no money, no job, and no fans like you promised!" I said. "And my best friend probably hates me!"

Vanessa lifted her head from the table. She reached over and patted my arm softly.

"J.D., I didn't mean for this to happen," she said. "Thank you for telling Mom the truth, by the way. I know that was scary."

We sat there without doing our math problems.

"And Jordan doesn't hate you," she said.

I hoped she was right.

Vanessa quickly opened up her math workbook when she heard Granddad pull into the driveway. I felt like making up my own word problems that would help me figure out how long it would take me to pay off Naija's camera. I closed my eyes and saw myself as an old, old man, older than Granddad, walking over to visit Naija, who was old, too, and handing him $500.

There had to be an easy way to get out of this. I just didn't know what it was yet.

CHAPTER 12
The Lifeline

Neither me nor Vanessa wanted to go outside after we finished our homework. I didn't even ask for computer time. What was there to look at? I brought out my sketchbook and started drawing pictures of dollar bills and sad faces, and Vanessa started cutting her doll's hair.

Granddad was getting in some TV time before his insurance visits later in the day. He only watched three types of television shows: the news, game shows, and soap operas. His favorite news anchor was Tom Frank, an older white man with salt-and-pepper hair who wore glasses and a black suit every day. After the local news ended on WTOK, Grand-dad watched *What's Up in the Southeast?*, a show that highlighted interesting people in Tennessee, Mississippi, and Georgia. His favorite segment was "Southeast Star." It was always hosted by this lady named Sharon McNeil, a Black woman who wore a pixie cut like my mom used to.

As soon as Ms. McNeil came on the screen, Granddad turned up the volume.

"This week's Southeast Star is the Jumping Jacks of Memphis, Tennessee!" A group of people who looked like they were in their twenties tumbled onto the set and threw each other into the air.

The three of us watched the Jumping Jacks' routine and interview after, where they talked about how they became expert gymnasts.

"I started tumbling at the age of three with my brother and sister, and now we travel the world as dancers," the smallest Jumping Jack, a man with dyed blond dreadlocks, said.

"That is truly unique!" Ms. McNeil said. "And how wonderful that you started at such a young age!"

She turned to the camera and continued. "And that's a perfect lead-in to our new contest: 'Southeast Star's Summer Vacation Showdown'!"

The screen faded to black behind her as she gave more details. "Hello, boys and girls between

the ages of five and twelve! Do you have a special talent or skill you think should be highlighted by 'Southeast Star'? Well, please visit our website and click the link for the Southeast Star competition. Follow the instructions, submit your video entry, and good luck! The winner will be invited to appear on our show, live in our studio! And they'll also receive a grand prize of five thousand dollars!"

Vanessa whipped around to look at me.

Whoa, here was my chance! I could pay back Naija without having to go back to Hart and Son, and become famous at the same time!

When I won the barber competition, I'd gotten written up in the *Meridian Star*. Now that I had learned some new things, like how to do girl hair and write a good video script, I knew I had a chance.

WE had a chance.

I thought about Jordan and how well he directed our videos. Jessyka was the only person who could edit a prize-winning video. And like the Jumping Jacks, me and Vanessa were an unstoppable brother-and-sister team. We had to get the group back together somehow.

CHAPTER 13
Parents Might Just Understand?

Not only would we need our friends' help to enter, but we'd need their parents' permission this time. Vanessa read the rules for "Southeast Star's Summer Vacation Showdown" to me on the website. They stated that each entry needed a parent or guardian to give permission for every minor to participate and to film a follow-up TV interview at WTOK.

Since neither one of us was going to go anywhere after we finished our homework that Monday, we decided we'd try to talk to Jessyka and Jordan. We agreed that Vanessa would talk to Jessyka and I would talk to Jordan, even though I was afraid that he wouldn't want to talk to me.

"He can't be that mad," Vanessa said. "He's the one who showed you the camera, plus you can tell him that we'll split the money evenly if we win. That way, he doesn't have to worry about his allowance."

I had a feeling Jordan would like that deal. $5,000 divided by 4 people was $1,250.00 each. That was a lot! Even after paying off the $500, he'd still have $750 left over.

I went next door to Jordan's house and knocked. My heart pounded so loud, I wondered if Mr. Mathews would be able to hear it when he opened the door.

"Hello, J.D.," he said. "Jordan's outside in the carport if you're looking for him. I told him he could not play video games for two weeks as part of his punishment for the camera."

"Oh," I said. I was sure Jordan was not in a good mood.

I found Jordan drawing with chalk on the ground.

"Hey, Jordan," I said cheerfully.

"Why are you so happy, J.D.?"

I knew Jordan wasn't going to let me ignore everything that happened with the football. I had to be honest, just like Mom had said.

"Look, Jordan, I'm sorry about what happened

at Jessyka's. We both messed up, and we're both paying for it. I just want to be best friends again. I have a plan to get us back to having a great summer," I said.

Jordan looked up. "Really?"

I told him about "Southeast Star" and the prize money to pay for the camera and the TV interview and how Vanessa was trying to get Jessyka to join, too.

"All you have to do is ask your dad to give you permission to enter the video contest with us," I added.

"I want to do this, J.D., but I don't know what my dad will say," Jordan said. "He's still mad. Let me try to ask him right now. You can stay out here. I'm not allowed to have any friends inside yet."

I watched Jordan jog back into his house, the screen door slamming behind him.

While I waited, I picked up a piece of chalk and wrote the word WINNER, just like I had done on the back of a kid's head to win the Great Barber Battle. I thought about how close I was to being a winner again.

Jordan came sprinting back outside not too long after with a big smile on his face.

"My dad said yes! With the money we're gonna win, we can buy our OWN camera!"

We jumped up and down with our fists in the air, one step closer to our dream!

When I got back to the house, Vanessa filled me in on her phone call with Jessyka. She said Jessyka had sounded tired when she picked up the phone. She had just gotten back from tennis camp for the day, where she had been training for a tournament next week. Mr. Fleet had lectured her all the way home about working harder because she'd missed so many balls.

"She doesn't like tennis camp," Vanessa told me. "Do you know what she said? She missed some of those balls on purpose. I think she wants to get kicked out."

In all the time I'd known Jessyka, I'd never known her to do badly on purpose. This sounded serious.

"I told her it was the perfect time to talk to her dad about 'Southeast Star,'" Vanessa said. "I pretended to be her dad, and Jessyka practiced what she wanted to say."

Jessyka had said a lot, and she ended by saying she could only be the best Jessyka, not the best Mr. Fleet, and that she hoped her dad could understand why she wanted to do "Southeast Star" instead.

"I'd say yes if I were Mr. Fleet," Vanessa said.

We didn't hear from Jessyka until after dinner.

Vanessa hung up the phone, and the grin on her

face told me that Jessyka had finally gotten what she wanted.

We told Mom that Jessyka's and Jordan's parents gave their permission to let them enter the contest with us.

"That's nice, kids," Mom said.

"Jessyka is finishing up editing our last video so we can send that one to 'Southeast Star.' I gave her your work email, Mom. Will you help us send it tomorrow?"

"The mornings are hectic, Vanessa, but sure. I can tell you kids have worked hard to make amends."

We were so close! It was going to be very hard to sleep that night.

CHAPTER 14
A Hope and a Prayer

"Kids," Mom said as we ate breakfast the next morning. "I got an email from a Mini Triathlete Jess."

My heart started to race. Jessyka had finished on time!

"Mom can you open it now?" Vanessa asked.

"Well, the file is huge!" Mom said. "I have to download it from a link Jessyka sent. I don't know if it will load before I have to go to work, Vanessa."

Granddad put down his coffee. "What are you talking about, may I ask?"

"Granddad, remember when they announced on 'Southeast Star' that they were accepting kids' talent for the next round of submissions? Well, me and Vanessa are going to enter! We have been doing hair on camera all summer," I said. I left out the part about wanting to win $5,000 to pay back the money I owed for Naija's camera.

"Oh, I love 'Southeast Star,'" Grandma said. "It reminds me of when I used to do ceramics segments for the morning show in Meridian. Sometimes I was even a guest on the morning show in Jackson, after all the kids were out of the house. I was big time!" Grandma laughed.

"Yes, Granddad, if we win, you can meet Sharon McNeil!" I hoped that would make him excited, too.

Granddad laughed to himself and then shot me a look over his mug as he took a sip of coffee.

"You kids sure got up to a lot these last few weeks without me knowing much," he said.

Mom came back into the kitchen to tell us the video had finished downloading.

"It's only a few minutes. Why don't we go watch it together?" she said.

Everybody broke out into smiles as they watched me and Vanessa onscreen. Justin kept trying to replay the part that showed him. He couldn't stop laughing!

"Okay, everybody, let's get this off so I can go to work," Mom said.

And with one click, our lives could change forever.

CHAPTER 15
Win, Lose, or Draw

The next day at breakfast, all I could think about was what I would wear if we won. I'd probably borrow some clothes from Jordan. How would I cut my hair? My usual fade, or should I try something new? We had sent our entry on the last day of the contest, so we didn't have long to wait before the winner was announced two days later.

"J.D., it's in God's hands, now," Granddad said.

"What's meant for you will be yours," Grandma added.

I knew my grandparents were trying to get me to put the contest out of my mind, but it didn't work.

Then mom reminded me what day it was.

"Are you ready for Take your Son to Work Day, J.D.?" she asked. "Exciting, isn't it?"

I had completely forgotten because of the contest. She'd mentioned it weeks ago. I wasn't sure what would be so exciting about the mayor's office, but I was happy I'd have somewhere to go while I waited for "Southeast Star."

Vanessa decided to go to the rec center with Grandma and take a ceramics class, probably with the same thought, so we all piled into the car for a change.

Grandma, Vanessa, and Justin, who was too young to go with us, got dropped off first, and then Granddad dropped me and Mom off at the mayor's office.

The mayor's office was in a building in the main square downtown. It was big and reminded me of pictures I'd seen of The White House in Washington, D.C.

Everyone greeted Mom as she walked through the door, wearing her usual work clothes: a white button-down shirt, a long black skirt, and low heels that clicked on the marble floors.

Mom had her own desk, and as soon as she got settled in and turned on her computer, the mayor walked in.

"Good morning, Mayor Thompson," she said. "Meet my son, James."

"Ah, yes, the famous barber!" Mayor Thompson replied.

It made me feel so good that he knew I cut hair!

Mayor Thompson was a tall, light-brown-skinned man with a bald head and a goatee. He had a pair of glasses pushed up onto his head that he lowered when he got an alert on his phone. He said it was good to meet me and excused himself.

I spent the rest of the day drawing on a pad of paper that had the mayor's office seal on it. I kept drawing me and my friends on television, receiving a check for $5,000 from Sharon McNeil. There was a big sofa in the office, where I sat and watched Mom answer phones, go over the mayor's schedule, and pop in and out of meetings. She asked me to follow her to a few of them, but I only understood the one about budgets—I didn't know what a "surplus" was, but I sure knew about "debt" right now.

My favorite part of the day was lunch, when I went to the office cafeteria and sat next to Mom the whole time. It was just like the alone time we

had when she used to cornrow my hair, before I started cutting it myself.

I wondered if Vanessa, Jessyka, and Jordan were as nervous as I was about the results of the contest. Maybe Vanessa would be, but probably not Jessyka or Jordan.

What would I do if we lost? Would Vanessa and my friends be disappointed in me? I'd know soon enough.

CHAPTER 16
Did We Win?

RING RING RING!

We'd been waiting for the phone to ring all day, and so far, it had been nothing but false alarms. An internet company had called to see if we were happy with our service. Two automated calls had come through, too. Granddad was sick of them! So when the phone rang for a fifth time, we let Mom pick it up.

"Hello," she said.

A few seconds later, Mom put her hand over the receiver and mouthed to us, *It's 'Southeast Star'!*

"I sure will. Thanks for calling," we heard her say.

"Well, Mom, what did they say?"

I didn't know how great my mom was at playing it cool until today. She could win a poker tournament!

Finally, she told us that she had spoken to the

segment's producer. They had reviewed just under one hundred submissions from kids with all sorts of unique talents. Of those kids, they had chosen our team as . . . second-prize winners.

What?!?

My face fell to the ground. I didn't remember anything about a second prize. I had been sure if they called the house, it was because we were the winners.

I looked at Vanessa, and she seemed crushed. How would we tell Jessyka and Jordan? They were counting on this, too.

Mom cleared her throat, and we both looked up at her.

"Nah, just kidding!" she said. "Your video won, and they want you to tape a live interview!"

I was too excited to be mad at Mom for her sneaky trick, and so was Vanessa. We joined in a group hug and jumped up and down.

Granddad walked in to see what was going on.

"Did someone win the lottery and didn't tell me?" he asked, joining our hug.

"No, Granddad, we are going to be on 'Southeast Star' doing hair!

"Oh my goodness, kids, that's my favorite show after *The Young and the Restless!*" he said. "Do you think you can get me a cameo?"

"Only if you let me cut your hair on live TV, Granddad," I said.

"Slow down there, son. I don't know about all that!"

CHAPTER 17
Big Time

Vanessa and I split up so we could tell our friends the good news. I couldn't wait to see my best friend. I rushed next door and asked Mr. Mathews if he'd let me talk to Jordan. He motioned for me to come in when I told him it was about "Southeast Star."

Jordan was in his room, separating and lining up his sneakers by brand.

"Hey, Jordan! Guess what?" I said excitedly. "We're going to be on TV!"

He set down a pair and looked up in disbelief.

"Are you serious?" he said.

"Yes, for real!"

"Wow," he said. "So I can finally stop paying my allowance to Naija?"

I explained that not only could he pay off Naija, he'd have more than enough money for the latest retros that were due to drop.

"Oh, that's gonna be sweet," he said. "But now I need to think about what I'm gonna wear to the show...."

"That's easy to fix," I said, leading the way to Jordan's closet.

CHAPTER 18
The Road to Jackson

The day of the interview, I made sure I woke up extra early to perfect my fade. I even cut a half moon part into my head. My hair had to look perfect.

Jordan had let me pick through his clothes and shoes. Even though he was bigger than me, he saved his sneakers from years past, and I ended up borrowing a pair of all-black Nike Air Max 720s and a white T-shirt with a black Swoosh on the front. I was going to look great on TV!

We told everyone we knew to watch. I called my dad. Xavier and Eddie even planned to watch at Eddie's house and invite some of the peewee football team over.

Granddad had agreed to drive me, Vanessa, and Jordan to the TV station in Jackson, which was an hour away. Jessyka and her dad were going to follow behind us in their car.

Granddad was the only adult free at the time to take us, but I think he just wanted to meet Sharon McNeil! He even put on a three-piece suit.

Vanessa went all out with her hair. She added colorful shapes using stencils and matched them with the colors on her skirt.

We tried to keep ourselves busy in the car by pretending to interview each other in the back seat.

"Hi, everybody, I'm Sharon McNeil!" Vanessa said, putting up her fist to her mouth like it was a microphone.

"Mr. J.D., what's your secret to a great haircut?" she asked me in a fake deep voice.

"I make it look great every time! You never have to worry if you're in my chair. You will come out looking fresh for days," I said.

Jordan burst out into laughter.

"I hope you don't say that on TV," he said.

"Why, what's wrong with that answer?" I asked him. "It's the truth."

"I dunno, man, maybe you should say something more exciting like, 'I may make every kid in Meridian look smooth, but now I'm taking on the state!'"

Vanessa's fake microphone fell in her lap when Jordan said that.

I remembered the Great Barber Battle and how that was my first time getting up in front of the whole town to show people what I could do. Now we'd be doing that in front of strangers from three states. I could tell that thought made Vanessa nervous. She hadn't done something like the Great Barber Battle. This was new for her.

"It's okay if you're nervous, Vanessa," I said. "Did you know that Mom used to feel like throwing up before her track meets? And that she was afraid of drawing people's blood when she was a nurse?"

Vanessa shook her head.

"Well, Mom says when we're nervous, we should imagine that everyone is cheering us on."

I think Mom's advice helped Vanessa, because her shoulders relaxed and she brought up her fake microphone again.

"So, J.D., tell us how your big sister has influenced your life," she said in her deep interviewer voice.

We all laughed, including Granddad.

CHAPTER 19
Showtime!

Once we arrived at the station, we were greeted by Kat McDonald, the lady Mom had spoken to on the phone.

Kat McDonald had the back of her head shaved, with diamonds cut into the base and the top pulled up into a set of dreadlocks with purple tips.

"Wow! How long did it take for you to get your hair like that?" I asked her.

"Eh, only about thirty minutes for the back and about an hour and a half for the color," she said.

I wondered if I could get any of my friends to let me loc their hair. I bet Jessyka would.

Kat wore a Tuskegee University T-shirt tucked into flared jeans. She explained she was going into her senior year and hoped to be an on-air personality one day.

"I'm so excited you agreed to do this! This is the

first segment I'm producing on my own," she said.

Kat gave us a quick tour of the studio. Jordan got to stand behind the cameras, and Vanessa saw where the anchors got their hair and makeup done.

Then I heard the loud click of high heels, and there was Sharon McNeil!

"Hello! So you're J.D. the Kid Barber, Vanessa Does It All, and their friends Jessyka and Jordan?" she asked.

Sharon was wearing a bright-pink pantsuit with matching pink heels. She looked like a giant crayon.

"Yes, ma'am," we said.

"You're all such little stars. I can see a bright future for you. We are so excited to have you here today! Kat will get you prepped for the segment. Remember, it's live, so there won't be any do-overs!"

Kat walked us into what she called the "green room," but there wasn't any green at all. It was just a regular room with an oversized couch, two chairs, a bathroom, and a table with a spread of food. It was more than I could imagine anyone eating, from fruits to cheeses to little pieces of bread and meat.

It reminded me of the New Meridian Buffet, but I was too nervous to eat.

There were photographs of famous people from Mississippi and the rest of the south on the wall. Oprah Winfrey was in the middle.

Vanessa, Jessyka, and Jordan ran for the couch and started to jump on it.

"Get down, kids!" Granddad said. "Have a seat, and stop showing out in front of these nice people!"

Kat chuckled to herself.

"I know this is exciting, but try to keep the room neat for our next guests," she said.

Kat clipped a microphone battery to everybody's waist, ran the cord up our backs, and clipped the microphone to the inside of our collars. Jessyka was wearing pink-and-black track pants with shiny black dress shoes and a white T-shirt tucked in. She had done her nails in matching alternating colors, and even her beads were color-coordinated. The night before, Jordan had me give him a new fade, with the letter J shaved on the side, and he had on a brand-new pair of red-and-black Air Jordan 1s.

"This is your microphone," Kat said. "Just speak

in your normal voice, and everything will be fine."

Kat explained that our segment would be no more than five minutes and that I would talk about what inspired me to start cutting hair, and Vanessa would talk about where she gets her ideas for different hairstyles and nail designs. Then Sharon would ask both Jordan and Jessyka a question about video production.

"You know all about us, Ms. McDonald!" I said.

"Please, call me Kat, and it's my job to know everything. I'm a producer!"

After the interview, Kat told me I would do a quick trim and style of the model's hair. The model was the weatherman, Carl "Stormy" Anthony. Vanessa would do Sharon McNeil's nails.

"Oh, that's exciting, J.D. I love Carl, too," Granddad said.

Granddad watched the news so much, it seemed like he was a fan of everyone at the station.

"We will knock on your door five minutes before your on-air appearance," Kat said. "And finally, don't forget to bring your tools out with you. We will have a stool for you so you can reach Carl's head."

I had brought one pair of clippers, sheers, and a comb, paste, and pomade. I hoped my equipment wouldn't stop working like it had during the Great Barber Battle.

Five minutes later, Kat told us it was showtime!

The four of us walked past the backstage area and stepped out onto the set. There was a couch, a desk, and cameras everywhere. My nerves began to kick in again. I think Vanessa noticed, because she put her hand on my shoulder.

"Hey there, J.D. the Kid Barber, right?" It was Carl. Carl was a middle-aged man with a few flecks of gray in his hair. He already had a cape on and wore glasses. I noticed that the back of his neck had not been shaped up.

"Hi, Mr. Anthony," I replied.

"Take it easy on me, now, my wife won't like it if I come back home with a crooked fade!"

I could relate. The crooked fade my mom gave me started my whole career.

Then I heard Kat's voice.

"Everyone, please sit on the couch now," I heard her say. It was weird to hear her voice without being able to see her. It was almost like we had walkie-talkies!

Then bright lights turned on, and I heard a little bit of music.

I took a deep breath. There was no live audience, but everyone in all of Mississippi, Tennessee, and Georgia would be tuning in!

Sharon McNeil walked out onto the stage, towering over us in her pink heels.

"We'll go live in three, two, one!" Kat said.

"Today, we are live with this week's Southeast Star, or Stars, I should say, except it's our junior edition! These fabulous young people not only do hair and nails, they make amazing videos to inspire us all at home!" Sharon McNeil said. "Now, each of you go down the line, and say your name and age," she finished before turning to face us.

"I'm J.D. the Kid Barber, and I'm eight years old!"

"I'm his older sister, Vanessa, and I'm ten."

"I'm Jessyka spelled with a *y* and a *k*, and I just turned nine!"

"I'm Jordan, and I just turned nine, too. We are

all going to be fourth graders next year, except Vanessa. She's in middle school."

"Amazing! I'm going to ask you each a question, and then we are going to have a surprise at the end," Sharon McNeil said.

"J.D. the Kid Barber, I understand you won a barber battle not too long ago? What inspired you to start cutting hair at your age?"

"Yes, ma'am. I beat the only real barber in town, Henry Jr. of Hart and Son. Then I started working for him. Hi, Henry Jr.!" I waved at the camera in case Henry Jr. was watching. "But I wanted a bigger audience, so I started putting videos online. Oh, and I started cutting my own hair because I didn't like the way my mom did it," I said.

Sharon laughed at that last thing I said. Vanessa gave me a look like I had told a family secret.

"By the way, it was fun driving to Jackson," I added. "I don't leave Meridian much!"

Sharon McNeil laughed again.

This wasn't so bad after all!

"And Ms. Vanessa, where do you get your ideas for your impressive nail art and hairstyles?"

"My own mind!" Vanessa said instantly. She hardly let Sharon finish her question! "I started this because it was a business idea for a school project. My brother is my employee. I bet I could teach the class after all I learned these last few weeks. Business is not easy!"

She always had to throw in that "my brother is my employee" line!

"Ms. Jessyka, my you look sporty! It's my understanding that you help shoot and edit these videos?"

"Yes, I am getting really, really good at both iMovie and Adobe Premiere. I can do moving graphics now, just like in movies," Jessyka said proudly.

"Wow, I can barely send emails on my cell phone!" Ms. McNeil said.

A few people in the crew laughed like they agreed with her.

"Now last, but not least, Mr. Jordan, what is your role in this project?"

"I am the director and equipment manager. I directed the video we used for the competition. I think I wanna direct my own movies one day. Or maybe my own video games. I don't know," Jordan said as he shrugged.

"Well, you certainly have time to figure that out and try lots of different options, and I wish you the best of luck with that!" Sharon said.

Kat's voice popped into my earpiece at that moment. "J.D., now stand on the stool that we put behind Carl!"

TV moved fast. We were almost done! It seemed much longer when you were just watching from home.

I stood on the stool behind the weatherman.

"What are you going to do for our brave weatherman today?" Ms. McNeil asked.

"I'm going to shape up the back of his head, spray some water on the top, and add pomade so it looks like he went to a real barber!" I said.

As I worked on Carl's head, Sharon McNeil asked me more questions.

"Who was your first client, J.D.?" she asked.

"My baby brother, Justin. Then my friend Jordan was next," I answered.

I heard Kat yell, "Thirty seconds to finish!" in my ear.

"So you can see I've cleaned the back of his

neck, spritzed the water, and added pomade. It's easy to do. Anybody can do it at home," I said.

I spun the chair around so Mr. Anthony could face all the cameras, and I saw a cameraman zoom in on the back of his neck.

I handed him a mirror.

"This is a job well done, J.D." he said.

Before the segment officially ended, Vanessa pulled out her stash of nail jewels and did a quick manicure on Ms. McNeil, adding a touch of color and bling.

"Look at how you completely transformed my nails, young lady! You really do Do It All!" Sharon said.

Kat told me and Vanessa to stand together for what she called our outro. I think that just meant saying goodbye to the folks watching at home.

"Tell everyone where they can find you, J.D. the Kid Barber, Vanessa Does It All, Jessyka the editor, and Jordan the director. Whiz kids, all of you!" Sharon McNeil said.

Vanessa didn't waste a second before she exclaimed, "Just look for our YouTube channel,

Kidz Cutz and Nailz! We do both girls' and boys' hair!"

The lights dimmed, and the camera people started walking away from the set.

As we walked offstage, the crew gave us pounds and fist bumps.

Kat appeared from behind the set.

"That was great, everyone! J.D., do you have an email address? I want to send you a copy of the segment after it airs," she said. "We'll also post it on the station's YouTube channel and tag you!"

That was music to my ears! WTOK had 150,000 subscribers. That's how many people would see the clip online if they tagged us!

"We don't have an email, but my mom does." I told Kat what it was.

"Thank you for making my first segment a success, kids!" Kat said.

The station sent us home with free T-shirts, water bottles, baseball caps, and PopSockets. I couldn't wait to pass them out to the people who have been there for me since the Great Barber Battle, like

Grandma, Justin, Mom, Xavier, Eddie, Henry Jr., and Henry Sr. I could even mail one to my dad!

Granddad said he was proud of what we had done. He kept bringing up his favorite parts of the interview while he drove me, Vanessa, and Jordan home.

"My grandchildren on television," Granddad said. "You kids let me know if you want help bringing in the senior market to your page. I've got ideas!"

I was proud, too, and my mind raced, thinking about what I could do next.

CHAPTER 20
Post-fame Life

It took a while for the $5,000 from the TV station to show up. But when it did, as promised, we split it four ways, and Naija was able to buy a new camera. Kidz Cutz and Nailz now had over 1,000 subscribers who tuned in every time we posted a new video. Our "Southeast Star" segment had done well and got almost 100,000 views on the WTOK YouTube channel! Finally, we were getting the kind of attention Vanessa and I had set out to get when we started our family business.

The contest was good for our friends, too.

Jessyka had a few more talks with her dad that led to some changes.

"Now I have one week a month where I get to decide by myself what I want to do with my time!" Jessyka said. "I write the letters J-E-S-S-Y-K-A across the whole week in the calendar!" Usually, she and Vanessa spent a lot more time doing videos for girl hair and nails.

"If I post every week, I'll keep getting new followers," Vanessa said.

"So are you still going to do Junior Business Scholars after this?" I asked her.

Vanessa shrugged.

"Maybe. I don't need the program to show I know how to run a business. I already learned on my own."

I guess she was right. She even had an employee. But I'd never say that out loud!

"I've got a lot of ideas, J.D. Watch out!"

Jordan was also excited about the future.

"I never thought I could win a contest," he said. "I'm not like you, J.D.! But I won anyway, so what else can I do?"

After talking it over with Naija, Jordan decided to start his own Twitch.

"What's Twitch?" Naija had asked.

"Don't worry about it," Jordan had said, smiling. "But I will need to borrow your camera again. . . ."

»»«««

Our segment was the talk of the town for days. Every time I went out, people had nice stuff to say. The same was happening online in the comments section. One day, when I was having my computer time, I looked through the comments on the video we submitted to WTOK to see what was new.

Most of them were regular compliments.

Those kids have mad skills!

Phew, look at the kid's cold fade!

But one was different—longer—and caught my eye.

Hi! I'm Holly Williams, the Director of Marketing and Sponsorship for the Beauty Brothers Hair Expo in Atlanta, Georgia. I'm interested in inviting J.D. the Kid Barber to our upcoming convention the first weekend in August! Last minute, yes, but please have a manager email me at hwilliams@beautybrothers.com. We would like to fully sponsor you.

Sponsor, what did that mean? I'd have to ask my mom.

Whatever it meant, a trip to Atlanta would be exciting! I wondered if Granddad would take me on a trip that far. I liked traveling to Jackson for the interview. Would my WTOK prize be enough to pay for a trip?

I'd never been to a hair expo. I'd heard Henry Jr. talk about one once. He'd told me that it was where people came together and taught each other new techniques, traded tips, and learned about new products and styles. I wanted to learn more, and maybe Holly Williams thought I could teach something, too.

The thing Atlanta made me think about most, though, was my dad. He lived in Atlanta. If I went to Atlanta for the hair expo, maybe I could visit him. If we drove, Atlanta was only four or five hours away. I knew that because we always passed by on our way to North Carolina to visit my uncle and cousins in Chapel Hill. Or maybe I'd take my very first plane ride!

I looked over to the sofa, where my mom was reading a book.

"Mom, can you come look at this, please?" I said.

"What is it, J.D.?" she asked.

"Do you think this is real?" I pointed to Holly's comment on the screen so Mom knew which one to read. "Can you email them to find out more?"

"I've certainly heard of Beauty Brothers," she said. "I can email them from work tomorrow."

Before I logged off the computer, I went on the Beauty Brothers website.

What I saw amazed me. There were videos of people getting the wildest hairstyles I'd ever seen! Different colors and designs I could have never dreamed of! There was a whole page describing the hair show. It was international, which meant the best barbers in the world would be there! And they wanted me to join!

Then came the most exciting part. There would be a featured act at the hair show, kid rapper Li'l Eazy Breezy!

"Mom! Li'l Eazy Breezy is performing at the hair show!" I yelled out.

Vanessa dropped the hair magazine she was

reading in the kitchen and ran over to the computer. "Where?!"

I showed her Holly's comment and the Beauty Brothers website. Vanessa started jumping up and down, and then I did, too.

"Who is Li'l Eazy Breezy?" Mom asked.

"He's the best kid rapper out," I said.

"Yeah, Mom, everybody knows his song, 'The TikTok Slide'!"

I pulled up the video for 'The TikTok Slide.' It had over 200 million views.

"Mom, can you PLEASE email back?" I asked.

"Tomorrow when I'm at work, J.D.," she said. "Have some patience."

By the time Mom got home from work, it felt like I'd waited eight years. She read me the email she got from Beauty Brothers.

Greetings, Ms. Jones,

I am Holly Williams, Director of Marketing and Sponsorship for the Beauty

Brothers Hair Expo. We are the largest beauty hair trade show in the Southeast region. Every year, thousands of haircare professionals across the globe flock to Atlanta, Georgia, to network, purchase exclusive beauty products, and gain continuous education within the haircare profession. This year, our theme is "The Digital GLAM Experience."

After watching your son's YouTube video, we are pleased to extend an offer to J.D. for sponsorship to this year's show in Atlanta. Sponsorship includes hotel and travel accommodations for your son and one adult chaperone. Both will receive complimentary meals, VIP access for the whole weekend, and an exclusive meet-and-greet with this year's featured act, internet sensation Li'l Eazy Breezy.

J.D. will be included in this year's Social Media Sensation category for the beauty industry. He will be invited to give a live demo onstage.

It's a great opportunity. We hope to see him there! Looking forward to hearing from you within a week if you'd like to attend.

All the best,

Holly Williams
Director of Marketing and Sponsorship, Beauty Brothers

P.S. Next year, our theme is "Natural Is Where It's At: The Best in Locs and Natural Haircare." We'll keep Vanessa in mind.

"Mom, you have to let J.D. go," Vanessa said. My sister had come through! All that time we spent together this summer had made a difference.

"Then me next year," she added, smirking after.

Mom read the email again in her head. "You know we make decisions as a family," she said.

It's true. All three grown-ups had to agree to something or it wasn't gonna happen.

"I'll discuss this with your grandparents."

I thought about how old I'd have to be to make my own decisions one day. Sometimes being eight was not so great.

Later that evening, I joined Grandma out on the porch. I didn't know if Mom had talked to her yet. It was warm out, and Grandma was watching Justin play with his toys before he had to take a bath.

"Grandma, have you ever been to Atlanta?" I asked.

"Yes, baby, once for a ceramics convention," she said.

"What did you think of it?"

"Well, it's definitely busy," she said. "A lot busier than Meridian. Almost TOO busy."

She laughed to herself and patted my back. "Why do you ask?"

"I think it's a place I would like to live when I get older," I said.

Grandma's eyebrows went up and she leaned back, like she hadn't expected my answer.

"Why's that?" she asked.